# SP[...] FFECTS
# [...] YOU

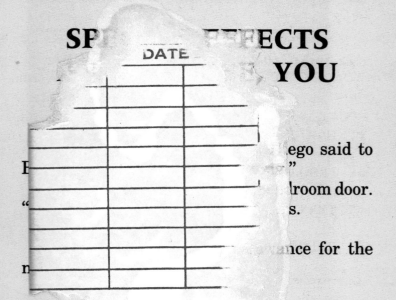

ego said to
"

room door.

s.

nce for the

Look for these other LUNCHROOM titles:

# THE FRENCH FRY ALIENS

## Ann Hodgman

Illustrated by Roger Leyonmark

## SPLASH™

A BERKLEY / SPLASH BOOK

# THE FRENCH FRY ALIENS

# Chapter One

# Oh, Oh, Oh

It was eleven-thirty on Friday morning. A cold rain was splattering against the windowpane. And Diego, like most of his sixth-grade classmates—except for Larry Watson, who was frankly snoring—was concentrating on the slow, slow, progression the clock's hands were making toward noon and lunch.

Eleven-thirty-one. Eleven-thirty-one and fifteen seconds. Eleven-thirty-two—

"And Diego, how would you like to play Tinker Bell?" Mrs. Doubleday suddenly asked.

*That* brought Diego back to life. "Pardon me, Mrs. Doubleday?" he asked in what he hoped was a nice, bright, alert voice.

His teacher grinned. "I thought that would get your attention! Honestly, Diego! Have you heard a word I've said in the last half hour?"

"Uhhh, not really," Diego confessed. He could feel his face getting hot. "I was, um, I was thinking about a new computer program I wanted to try at home. Sorry."

Mrs. Doubleday shook her head. "I'll start over. As *some* of you may have heard me saying, Mr. Haypence has come up with a fantastic idea to boost school spirit."

*Uh-oh*, Diego thought.

Mr. Haypence was the principal at Hollis Elementary School. He was always coming up with fantastic new ideas to boost school spirit. But what Mr. Haypence called a fantastic new idea was usually something that would make ordinary people wake up screaming in the middle of the night.

"As long as it's not another dance," Diego muttered to his best friend, Bob Kelly, who was sitting next to him. All the boys in the sixth grade were still wincing at the memory of the formal ballroom dance Mr. Haypence had forced on them a few weeks before.

"He wouldn't dare try *that* again," Bob whispered back. "And it's too soon for another fundraiser. Whatever his new idea is, though, it's going to be stupid."

"Mr. Haypence wants to start a new tradition here at Hollis," Mrs. Doubleday announced. "Class plays! Isn't that nice?"

Diego and Bob stared at each other in horror. Yes, this idea was really stupid.

"Each sixth grade will be assigned a play," Mrs. Doubleday went on, "and we'll all get a chance to perform it for our classmates, families, and friends. We'll sell the tickets ourselves, make the costumes ourselves, design the set ourselves, and—"

"And pass out the barf bags ourselves?" Diego whispered to Bob. "Nothing, Mrs. Doubleday," he added quickly when he saw his teacher's eye on him.

"Good," Mrs. Doubleday said. "Now, the play Mr. Haypence has chosen for us is a...a"— she paused for a second—"a very interesting and lovely version of *Peter Pan*. It's right in this book here." She picked up the battered red book on her desk and began leafing through it. *"One Hundred and One Wonderful Plays for Children!"*

Glancing around the room, Diego saw that he wasn't the only person eyeing the book suspiciously. *Any* book that had the words "for children" in the title needed to be handled with extreme care. You never knew when it would start breaking out into poems about cute little

3

itsy-bitsy kittens or the joy of seeing the first tulips of spring. . . .

"Just let me find the page I want," Mrs. Doubleday murmured. "Oh, here it—"

*Whump!* The book tipped out of her hands and fell heavily to the ground.

"I hope that's not an omen," whispered Diego.

"You don't think she'll really make us memorize lines, do you?" Tiffany Root asked as she set down her lunch tray at the table where Diego, Bonnie Kirk, Bob, and Chantilly Lace were sitting.

"Probably," Diego replied. "That's usually what you do in plays."

Tiffany was the sixth grade's biggest worrier. She was the kind of person who actually got upset over stuff like whether germs get hurt if you stepped on them. Now her eyes widened in horror. "But I'll get horrible stage fright!" she wailed. "I know it! I won't be able to remember anything, and then my throat will close up, and I won't be able to breathe, and—"

"Cheer up," said Bonnie Kirk, rolling her eyes at Diego. In Diego's opinion, Bonnie was one of the few really sensible girls in Mrs. Doubleday's class. "If you can't talk, Mrs. Doubleday won't pick you for a part. Then you won't have anything to worry about."

"Except feeling left out!" said Tiffany mournfully. "Imagine how I'll feel! Watching the rest of you up on stage while I sit in the foothills, or headlights, or whatever they're called, wishing and *wishing* I were up there sharing in your glory. My throat all closed up..."

"Since your throat's closed, can I have your french fries? Mrs. Carlson wouldn't let me have any more." The speaker was Rocky Latizano, the class's—and maybe Pasadena's—biggest eater. He plunked down a tray piled with enough food to feed an entire troop of construction workers: a huge mound of cheeseburgers, baked beans, potato salad, and banana bread. With a satisfied sigh, he pulled out his chair, tilted back his head, picked up the baked beans, and began using his fork to shovel them into his mouth at top speed. Everyone else at the table quickly averted their eyes.

"Rocky, you're *so* disgusting," Chantilly groaned.

"But, what about this play thing? Are we going to be putting it on here in the lunchroom?" Bonnie wanted to know.

"Where else?" Diego asked. "Mr. Haypence

loves this lunchroom so much he probably sends it valentines!"

He tipped his chair back and stared around the Hollis lunchroom. It was certainly something to see. It had been built over the summer. Mr. Haypence had been in charge of decorating it, and he hadn't left anything out. Of course, there were a few things it might have been *better* for him to have left out—like the gleaming chrome peanut-butter spreader, which looked like a torture device and was so complicated and dangerous to operate that none of the cafeteria workers would touch it. But Mr. Haypence was actually right for once when he said there wasn't another lunchroom like this one in all of Pasadena.

Diego turned to look in the direction of the stage that ran along one end of the lunchroom. It was covered with an electric-blue velvet curtain—another one of Mr. Haypence's special touches. "Yes, that's where we'll take our bows," he said glumly. "I can see you now, Bob. Standing up there in your Peter Pan suit...I mean flying up there—"

"Hey, what are you talking about? *I'm* not going to be—" Bob began.

"Oh, yes you are," Diego interrupted. "And Chantilly's going to be Wendy, in a big old grandma-type nightgown. And there you'll be swooping back and forth through the air, shouting about how you believe in fairies.... Oh, it's going to be beautiful. I can't wait to see it."

When they got back to the classroom, Mrs. Doubleday announced that it was Diego she wanted to read the part of Peter Pan.

"It's just a reading!" she said when Diego turned pale. "We won't necessarily be sticking with these parts. I only want to hear how the play sounds. Come on, Diego. Give it a try, okay? Chantilly, you can be Wendy. We'll pick up the other parts as we go along."

Diego darted a glance at Chantilly. She looked just as anxious as he was. Chantilly was new in school. For a while she had had trouble fitting in, but now everyone liked her.

Everyone else in the class settled back in their seats as Diego and Chantilly dragged themselves to the front of the room. "I'm really looking forward to *this*!" Bob said in a wickedly cheerful voice as Mrs. Doubleday passed out the scripts.

Diego picked up his script and cleared his throat. He could hardly believe what was happening to him. *If this is just a reading*, he thought, *I'll read as badly as I can. I'm going to make sure I don't get stuck with this part!*

It was kind of hard to read the first word badly, since that word was "Oh." But Diego did his best.

"Oh, oh, oh," he read haltingly. "What fun it is to fly. What fun it is to be Peter Pan. I love to fly with my friends on the island of Never-Neverland. We have all kinds of adventures. But there is one thing we do not have. And that one thing is a mother...."

Bob Kelly buried his face in his hands, and his shoulders began shaking with laughter. *What a ratfink*, Diego thought vengefully. *Some best friend!*

Diego put his script down. "Uh, Mrs. Doubleday, are you sure this is the right play?" he asked as politely as he could. "It seems ... well, a little young for us."

"Oh, we can jazz it up as we go along," Mrs. Doubleday said breezily. "Keep going."

Diego forced himself to pick up his script again. "I feel so lonely that I think I will go flying," he read in a dull monotone. "Oh, oh, oh. Here is a house. A big house. I see a girl inside! I wonder if she could be a mother for me! I will knock on the window and see. Knock! Knock!"

Chantilly gave Mrs. Doubleday a desperate look that screamed "Help!" and cleared *her* throat. "Who could that be?" she asked, staring fiercely at her script. "I do not think it is John or Michael. They are in bed."

"And besides, they don't go flying around knocking on the outside of windows," Rocky Latizano yelled from the back of the classroom.

Chantilly's lips twitched, but she kept her eyes glued to her script. "I will go to the window and see," she said, her voice becoming as flat and expressionless as Diego's. "Oh, oh, oh! It is a boy! A boy dressed in green! Come in, boy! Can you teach me how to fly?"

And on and on it went—for page after page after page. Flying. Talking to Tinker Bell. Fighting with Captain Hook. All the old, familiar Peter Pan adventures were there. But they were all written in a language that sounded as though it had been run over by a car. A big car.

At last, Mrs. Doubleday said, "Thanks, guys. You did a great job. And I think—if it's okay with the rest of the class—that I'd like Chantilly and Diego to keep their parts. Would anyone mind?"

A wave of pure relief washed over Diego as he saw a hand go up in the back of the room. Then his spirits sank again. The hand belonged to Jennifer Stevens. She couldn't possibly want his part.

Jennifer tossed her hair over her shoulder.

"Don't you think we should at least have casting calls, the way they do in the movies?" she said, pouting. "Maybe some of us other girls might like to be Wendy. I mean, she probably gets to wear the best outfits and everything...."

"I'd be happy to have tryouts for Wendy if lots of girls are interested in the part," Mrs. Doubleday said. "And how about you, boys? Anyone else want to be Peter?"

Diego looked around the room eagerly, but there were no takers.

"Well, I guess it will be you, Diego," said Mrs. Doubleday. Diego's face fell. "And I know you're going to do a fabulous job," Mrs. Doubleday said soothingly. "Now, that's enough play for a while. Let's get back to work. Everyone take out your social studies folders. Remember? Today we're starting our unit on favorite foodstuffs around the world. Rocky, tell me why..."

*Oh, oh, oh,* thought Diego as he slid back into his seat. *This is not going to be any fun at all.*

*If only I did know how to fly. I'd be out of here before you could say "fairy dust."*

## Chapter Two

# Peter Pan Goes on Strike

"Diego, I'm not kidding! You'd better get down here!" Mrs. Lopez called up the stairs on Monday morning.

Sometimes it seemed to Diego that he and his parents spent half their time shouting up and down the stairs at each other. "I'll be there in a sec!" he called back. "I just want to finish this one little thing!" His fingers skittered across his computer keyboard.

"*No more things!*" his father shouted from the breakfast room. "The bus leaves in nine minutes!"

"Let it leave," Diego muttered to himself. "I don't want to be on it anyway. I just want to stay in my room for the rest of my life."

If you had to pick one room to spend the rest

of your life in, Diego's would have been a good one. As long as you planned to be some kind of science genius, that is.

One whole side of the room was taken up by Diego's computer stuff: monitor, disk drive, keyboard, printer, an entire bookcase full of disks, a messy stack of computer manuals, printer ribbons, different kinds of computer paper, and scrawled bits and pieces of paper that Diego kept meaning to organize someday.

Another wall was lined with experiments in progress. Since some of the experiments had to do with animals whose life cycles Diego was observing, that section of the room tended to get a little smelly. No one in Diego's family really minded; both of his parents were science teachers, and his six-year-old brother, Carlos, loved animals. But visitors to the Lopez house had been known to wrinkle their noses and ask if the refrigerator was working okay.

The third wall of Diego's room was all bookcases, all of which were filled to overflowing. The wall by the door was covered with diagrams illustrating some math projects that Diego had worked on at the university last summer.

"Hey, D! Whatcha doing?"

Diego sighed. "Hi, Carlos." Unfortunately, Carlos *never* avoided Diego's room. He kept coming back to it as though it exerted some kind of magnetic force on him. No matter how Diego was feeling, no matter how grumpy he acted, no matter how clear he made it that he wanted to be left alone, Carlos stayed, hanging around and staring at Diego like an eager puppy. And Carlos was *always* in a good mood. It could get tiring, especially on mornings like this one. When you're trapped inside a really bad mood, the last thing you need is some re- lentlessly cheerful person hanging around and getting in the way—even if, *especially* if, that person happened to be your baby brother.

"I'm just writing this program," Diego mut- tered, staring fixedly at the monitor.

"Hey, neat!" chirped Carlos. "What kind of program?"

"You wouldn't understand it," Diego said. "It's not in regular English."

"I bet I'd understand if you explained it to me!" Carlos said. "I bet I would, D! Please! Please tell me about it? C'mon, D!" He was bouncing up and down with excitement.

"Maybe later." Diego stood up abruptly and switched off the monitor. "We should go down for breakfast now."

"Don't turn it off!" Carlos protested. "How 'bout if I bring up some breakfast for you on a tray? Then you can show me how to write a program! How 'bout it? Huh, D?"

For the first time that morning, Diego smiled. "Carlos," he said, "you've actually done the impossible. You've made me *want* to go to school."

Not that the feeling lasted long.

"Oh, oh, oh!" Rocky Latizano bellowed as Diego got off the school bus. Everyone outside the school turned to see what was going on. "It is Peter Pan. Hello, Peter! Why are you walking instead of flying? Where is Wendy? Will you fight big, mean Captain Hook today? Oh, oh, oh. Scary, scary!" And he burst into maniacal laughter.

A few minutes later, as Diego was taking his books out of his locker, Jennifer came marching up. "I've been thinking it over," she said importantly. "And I've decided I'd rather design the costumes for this play than be Wendy. You know, I *really* have a feel for fashion. Everybody says so. And I, like, plan to be, like, a big-time fashion designer. Anyway, here's my sketch for your costume."

"Costume?" Diego said.

"You're Peter Pan, remember?" Jennifer reminded him. In fact, it seemed as if no one was ever going to let him forget it.

"Oh, yeah." Diego took the sketch from her hand. Then he bit back a yelp of pure horror.

"I thought the regular Peter Pan was bad!" he said to himself. "But *this* . . ." Words failed him.

In Jennifer's design, Peter Pan was shirtless. And he was wearing what could only be called a skirt. It was made of leaves, but it was still a skirt. And the braided thing around the head—was it supposed to be made of grass?—looked more like a halo than anything else. He was wearing leather sandals, too, with straps that tied at the knee. *Had Jennifer gotten those from Greek paintings?* Diego wondered.

"I didn't want to, like, just do the regular old Peter Pan," Jennifer explained. "I wanted something a little different, something with a little zip, you know?"

"This certainly is different," Diego said carefully. "Only, it might—it might be sort of hard to move around on stage in it, don't you think?"

"Well, you won't really be moving that much," Jennifer said blithely. "You'll be strapped into some kind of wire thing to fly you around. I haven't designed that yet."

*Why is everyone so sure I'm going to be flying for this play?* Diego thought uneasily. "Uh . . . yeah," he said aloud. "But, Jennifer . . . excuse me for mentioning this, but what am I supposed to wear under this skirt thing? Those leaves look kind of . . . see-through."

Jennifer wrinkled her nose. "Don't be gross, Diego. That's up to *you*! I can't go around designing *every* part of your costume!" Then she turned and began walking down the hall.

"Wait!" Diego called. "You forgot your sketch!"

"Oh, I don't need it," Jennifer's voice drifted back to him. "I've already shown it to Mr. Haypence."

"And did he . . ." Diego couldn't bring himself to finish the question. He was too sure of what the answer would be already.

"Oh, he really loved it! He said it would make Peter Pan a really, like, original production. 'Very much in keeping with our lunchroom.' Those were his exact words! See you in class!"

With a sinking heart, Diego watched her go. "So Haypence likes that costume," he said to himself. "Good. Let *him* wear it. Because *I'm* not going to."

Diego squared his chin resolutely. "What I *am* going to do," he vowed, "is go on strike!"

"Okay, people," Mrs. Doubleday said later that afternoon. "Let's try the scene where Captain Hook and Peter have their big fight. Who'd like to be Captain Hook? Rocky? Give it a try from the top of page twenty-six."

Rocky picked up his copy of the script and swaggered to the front of the classroom. "'Now I, Tiger Lily, will...'" he began. "Tiger Lily? That can't be right. Oh, yeah, page *twenty*-six. Okay, here it is."

"'Ah-hah! You are my bad, bad, enemy, Peter!'" he read enthusiastically. He swished an imaginary sword through the air. "'Now I must feed you to the crocodile. What do you have to say about that?'"

Diego just stood there, staring into space.

"Uh, Peter?" Rocky leaned forward and nudged him in the side. "What are your last words before I feed you to the crocodile?"

Diego didn't say a word. He only smiled faintly, as though he were listening to far-off music.

"Come *on*, Diego!" Rocky bellowed impatiently. "The crocodile! The crocodile!"

"Have you lost your place, Diego?" asked Mrs. Doubleday kindly. "We're at the top of—"

"No, I haven't lost my place," Diego calmly interrupted. "I just can't read this."

Mrs. Doubleday looked puzzled. "Can't *read*

it? Is there something the matter with your eyes?"

Diego shook his head.

"Then what's the trouble?" his teacher asked.

Diego just stared at her. Mrs. Doubleday was usually pretty smart. Why couldn't she understand this?

"I'll tell you why I can't read it," he said. "It's unbelievably stupid." Students gasped at Diego's boldness, then giggled. "I'll give you a few examples," Diego continued.

"Page twelve. 'I need a mother. Every boy wants a mommy to take care of him.'

"Page twenty-one. 'Oh, oh, oh. I hope that the pirates will not be mean to us!'

"Page fifty. 'Oh, Tinker Bell! How pretty your wings look! I wish I had pretty wings!'"

Diego slammed the script shut. "Mrs. Doubleday, that's not a play for sixth-graders! It sounds like a first-grade reading book! How can I read moronic stuff like that out loud? Sixth-graders shouldn't have to talk about pretty fairies' wings! It's—it's—it's cruel and unusual punishment!"

For a second, Mrs. Doubleday stared at him in silence. Then, suddenly, she started to smile, and then she started to laugh.

"It *is* a totally ridiculous script, isn't it?" she

sputtered. "I'm sorry, Diego. I keep trying to think the best of it, but it really is impossible! I don't know what Mr. Haypence was thinking...."

Diego smiled at her. "So we don't have to do it?" he asked happily.

Mrs. Doubleday stopped laughing. "Oh, no," she said. "You still have to do it. But maybe we can find some way around the... around the ridiculousness."

"Why can't we really feed Captain Hook to a crocodile?" That was Louie Watson. He and his twin brother Larry, commonly known as the Human Demolition Team, could always be counted on for gory suggestions. "That would be more exciting than just *pretending* he's dead!"

"Yeah!" chimed in Larry, pounding his desk excitedly. "We could have a real plank, with real water. Maybe some piranhas, too..."

"Bor-ing," drawled Jennifer. "It would be a lot more interesting if we could work some fashion into this thing. Like, say, Peter and Wendy don't go back to Never-Neverland at all. Instead, they go to New York City and start this really cool design business—leather miniskirts, that kind of thing. That would be much more modern, don't you think?"

"I think that would be really stupid," bellowed Rocky. "I tell you what would work. Real food! Right on stage! They could have these enormous fights and—"

Mrs. Doubleday rapped on her desk. "Okay, gang, listen up!" she shouted. Gradually, the room quieted down. "I can see that you're all bursting with ideas," she continued. "So I'll tell you what I'm going to do. I'm going to turn this whole play over to you."

The heartfelt sighs of relief rushing out of twenty-four throats could have knocked down a brick wall.

"As long as the play stays *Peter Pan*—and I mean a *Peter Pan* that Mr. Haypence will recognize—you can do whatever you want with it," Mrs. Doubleday announced. "You can write it, produce it, and direct it all by yourselves. I'll be on hand if you need me. But only if you need me. And if your expenses go over the money Mr. Haypence has allotted, you'll have to come up with the extra."

"That can be my department," Junior said importantly. He pulled out a little black notebook and jotted something down in it.

"But who will be in charge?" Tiffany cried shrilly. "If no one's in charge, everyone will fight and—"

"How about Diego?" suggested Mrs. Doubleday. "I think he can handle it, don't you?" She smiled at him.

Diego grinned back. "I think so," he told her.

"As long as I don't have to wear a skirt," he said to himself, "I can handle anything."

# Chapter Three

# The Search for Peter

"'...So Peter Pan and Captain Hook decide to make friends instead of fighting,'" Tiffany Root read aloud. "'They shake hands and promise to be nice all the time and never to argue again. Meanwhile, the rest of the pirates become best friends with the Lost Boys. Peter still doesn't get any older, so when Wendy grows up, she and Captain Hook decide to get married and adopt him. And everyone lives happily ever after.'"

Tiffany looked up anxiously from the pink sheet of paper she was holding. "How does that sound?" she asked. "I wanted to make it less mean, you know? All that fighting is so up-

23

setting! Don't you think the play would be a lot better my way?"

At least two people in the audience didn't.

"Barf! *B-a-a-a-r-r-f!*" shouted Larry Watson. Then, as if they had rehearsed it, he and his twin brother Louie dropped out of their seats and began rolling around on the floor, making incredibly loud gagging noises.

"I don't think they like it, Tiffany," Jennifer Stevens said helpfully.

It was the day after Mrs. Doubleday had told her class they could put on their own version of *Peter Pan*. Diego had called an after-school meeting in the lunchroom to go over ideas for the play.

"So you don't like it . . . I mean, I thought it was a good idea . . . " she said faintly. Tiffany looked crushed by her resounding rejection.

*I'd better get this meeting under control*, thought Diego. *But how? It's not like I have any brilliant ideas.*

The Watson twins were still writhing on the floor. "Are you guys all done?" Diego asked them.

Larry raised himself up on one elbow. "I guess so," he said. "But wasn't that the barf-ingest idea you ever heard?"

"Let's drop it!" Diego said quickly. Tiffany flashed him a wet-eyed, grateful glance.

"Hey, listen, everyone," Diego said when the twins finally simmered down. "Instead of thinking about ways to change the story, maybe we should just add stuff to it."

"Add stuff? What kind of stuff?" Jennifer asked.

"Well, stuff we like. Take movies, for example. Has anyone seen any movies they really liked?"

*"The Blood Drinkers!"* shouted Rocky Latizano. "It's a great movie!" His eyes were shining. "You know that scene where Psycho Mike sticks out his claws and just *rips* that—"

"DON'T SAY IT!" screamed half the girls in the class.

Rocky held up his hands. "Okay! Okay! But why can't Captain Hook be a little more like Psycho Mike? I mean, who's scared of a plain old pirate? Captain Hook should be a total creep, the kind of guy who'll really terrify the audience. Get rid of all that jolly old yo-ho-ho stuff! Make him really *insane!*"

"That's a great idea," Chantilly said unexpectedly. "We should change Wendy, too. She's such a wimp. All she does is cook for the boys and get captured by the pirates. And why should a girl who's our age want to spend all her time being a *mother*? I think Wendy should be more like Peter."

"How about science-fiction movies?" Diego interrupted. "Is there anything we could steal from them?"

"Special effects," Bob said promptly.

A murmur of approval ran through the room.

"Maybe Never-Neverland could be a special kids' planet, not some dopey fairy-tale place," Bob continued. "Peter and Wendy and all the boys have to fight aliens there, not just pirates. And they have lots of high-tech weapons and things. They vaporize people, and—"

"That would be perfect!" Jonathan Matterhorn agreed enthusiastically. "I bet none of the other classes will do anything like that! Just think about it... They'll be putting on *Little Red Riding Hood*, and *we'll* be killing people with phasers!"

"Can we have holograms, too?" asked Junior Smith.

"Let's have man-eating plants!" someone else yelled.

"And, like, these weird floating aliens that burst into flames in midair!"

"And food that suddenly appears in your mouth without you having to pick it up!" That was Rocky's suggestion, of course.

"And we could have—"

"And a—"

"And—"

"Hold it!" called Diego. "I agree with you. That stuff would be perfect. In fact, it would be fantastic. But where are we going to *get* all those special effects? They're pretty expensive. They're also not the kind of thing you can buy at the drugstore, you know!"

There was a pause. A long, meaningful pause.

"Wait a minute," Diego said suspiciously. "Why are you all staring at me?"

"Well, *you're* the science genius," said Jonathan Matterhorn. "I'm sure you can come up with *something*." He turned to the rest of the kids. "Don't you think so, everyone?"

Yes. Everyone thought Diego could come up with something. A few floating aliens, a few holograms, a man-eating plant or two. No problem.

"All you have to do is twist a few wires together," Rocky assured him. "The rest of it you can do with lighting."

Then everyone decided that Chantilly was going to direct the play. Jennifer would design the costumes. (Diego managed to drop a couple of hints about making them a little more high-tech than skirts made of leaves.) And Tiffany would design the sets.

"Because I *am* very artistic, you know," Tiffany said. "Besides, I just know I'd throw up if I had to be on stage in front of zillions of people."

Diego, everyone agreed, would come up with the special effects. *And* he would write the play.

"It just makes more sense for you to do it!" Junior Smith explained. "How can anyone else write a plot when we don't know what kind of special effects you're going to come up with? It would be a waste of time. And time *is* money, you know!"

"But what about *my* time?" protested Diego. "I don't want to give up my whole life to Peter Pan!"

"I never should have done it," Diego said, gritting his teeth. "I never should have gone on strike. I should have said I loved that stupid play, and memorized those stupid lines, and worn Jennifer's stupid leaf skirt. And I would have felt a lot less stupid than I'm feeling now."

He rolled his chair back and stared at his computer screen. The bright green lines of dialogue he'd written twinkled mockingly back at him.

"Is it just my imagination," Diego asked

himself, "or is my script just as bad as the one in Mr. Haypence's book?"

It certainly seemed that way. None of the characters would do anything Diego wanted them to. Wendy sounded way too bossy, and Peter Pan was as peppy as a game-show host.

Captain Hook was the biggest problem. Diego had turned him into an android and made his hook a laser. He had taken all the "yo-ho-ho's" out of his dialogue and tried to replace them with something more sinister. But he had a funny feeling it wasn't working. "Zap, Peter Pan, zap, zap," didn't even sound as colorful as "yo-ho-ho." Maybe he should change it to "Sizzle, Peter Pan, sizzle, sizzle"?

Diego sighed. "That wouldn't scare me if I were watching this play," he muttered. "It would just make me—"

"Hey, D! What are you doing?"

Carlos was standing worshipfully at Diego's door in his pajamas.

"Oh, hi, Carlos," Diego mumbled. "I'm writing a play. *Trying* to write one," he corrected himself.

"A play! Wow! That's great! What's it about?"

"Peter Pan," Diego told him.

"Hey, he's my favorite person!" This was news to Diego. Right up until that second, Bat-

29

man had been Carlos's favorite person.

"Can I read what you've written?" Carlos came bouncing toward the monitor.

"No!" Diego threw himself in front of the screen. "Don't! It's too horrible! I—"

Then he stopped. *Carlos won't think it's stupid*, he thought. *He likes whatever I do. And maybe the play sounds better than it reads on the page* . . .

"Sure you can read it, Carlos," he said kindly. "In fact, how would you like to take one of the parts? I'll take another part, and we can read it out loud."

It certainly was easy to make Carlos happy. "You bet I'll read it with you!" he shouted. "What part should I take?"

"Well, why don't you be Captain Hook?"

"CAPTAIN HOOK!" Carlos whooped. "Hey, he's my favorite favorite person! Do I get to use my hook on anyone?"

"Well, not exactly. See, in my play he doesn't have a hook. He's got a laser that comes out of his wrist."

"A *laser*?" Carlos wrinkled his nose. "You don't call him Captain Laser, do you?"

"No, no. He's still Captain Hook."

"Well, he's still a *pirate*, isn't he?" Carlos asked suspiciously.

"N-not exactly," Diego said. He couldn't

meet his brother's accusing eyes. "He's sort of more like an android. You know, a robot..."

But Carlos was shaking his head. "Thanks, but I don't feel like reading that play with you. I'm going to go clean my room." Then he walked away.

"That does it." Diego switched off the computer. "I can't write any more of this." If even *Carlos* didn't like his idea...

He strode rapidly out of the room, picked up the phone, and dialed Bob's number.

"Listen, you've *got* to help me," he said when Bob got on the line. "I can't write this play. You've got to do it for me. Please!"

"But it's your idea. You should get the credit!" Bob said.

"Believe me, I won't get any *credit* if I write this," Diego said fervently. "I'll just get a lot of enemies. Please, Bob. You've got to do it. You've got to. If you don't, I'm going to build a plank and feed myself to that ticking crocodile!"

# Chapter Four

# Peter in Pasadena

"Diego! Bob's here!" Mrs. Lopez called up the stairs the next afternoon.

"Come on up, Bob!" Diego called back. In a second he heard Bob's tread on the stairs, and then his friend appeared in the doorway.

"Hi. Have you got the play?" Diego asked eagerly. "How did it come out?"

"Okay," Bob said. He sat down on Diego's bed and fanned himself with the three sheets of paper he was holding. "I'm not Shakespeare or anything, but I think it's pretty decent," he said.

"Is that, uh, all of it?" asked Diego. "I mean, I'm sure you did a great job, but it doesn't look very long to me."

"Oh, this is just a summary," Bob replied.

"I wanted to show it to you before I started working on the script." He handed the pieces of paper over and leaned back.

Diego picked up the first sheet and began reading.

"Planetary Peter Pan" was the title at the top of the page. Diego smiled when he saw it.

"What is it?" Bob asked nervously.

"It's a good title," Diego told him.

"Thanks." Bob relaxed again.

" 'The play is set nowadays,' " Diego read. " 'The Darling family lives in the suburbs of Pasadena.

" 'One day, Wendy, John, and Michael Darling are walking home from the school-bus stop when they see a dark shadow flitting around the back of their house. At first, they think it's a burglar, and they're frightened because they know no one is home.' "

"Where's Mrs. Darling?" asked Diego, looking up.

"Still at work," said Bob. "She doesn't come back until later."

"Well, wouldn't they have a babysitter or a housekeeper or something?"

"They still have that big dog Nana," said Bob. "Keep reading. You'll see where she comes in."

" 'The kids are too scared to go inside by

themselves, so they run around to the back of the house and let Nana out. Then all of them rush inside and up the stairs. Through Wendy's bedroom window they see there's a boy outside—and he's beckoning to them to let him in! He looks nice, so Wendy opens the window and he flies in. But no sooner is he inside than Nana grabs his shadow and tears it off. Frightened, the boy flies out the window again.'"

Once again, Diego frowned. And once again, Bob practically fell out of his chair asking what was the matter.

"Bob, cut it out!" Diego objected. "You're acting like a jack-in-the-box! I'm just wondering how I'm going to make that part about the shadow look real."

"Oh, I'm sure you can do it," said Bob breezily. "I'm not worried about that. The writing is the only thing that bothers me."

"I can see *that*," said Diego, grinning at him.

"'The next night after supper, the children are alone again—both Mr. and Mrs. Darling have to work late. Wendy has just gone to sleep when she hears a tapping at the window. It's Peter, with Tinker Bell! He's come back to look for his shadow. Wendy promises to give it back if he'll teach her and the boys how to fly.

"'He does teach them to fly, using some of Tinker Bell's fairy dust. In moments, the four kids and Nana are all flying around the room. . . .

"'. . . the four kids and Nana are flying around the room when they hear something downstairs. Their parents are home from work! Without a moment's thought, the three Darling kids and Nana follow Peter out the window.

"'The next scene shows them flying through the sky, chasing birds and playing with the stars. Then they come to the planet of Never-Neverland.

"'It's a wonderful place. You can have any kind of adventure you've ever dreamed of there—from laser battles with aliens to sword fights with pirates. And the worst villain on the island is the pirate Captain Hook.'"

"He's still a pirate, then?" Diego asked. "I turned him into an alien when I was trying to write the play."

"Yeah, he's still a pirate, but he's got supernatural powers," Bob explained. "Also, I decided to make him friends with some of the evil aliens on the planet. They come to his rescue whenever he needs them. You'll see— it's in the summary. I thought Peter and the other kids could have three different kinds of battles with Captain Hook. In the first, the aliens help him. In the second, he keeps changing into all these different shapes, and in the last one he and Peter have a sword fight."

"A sword fight, huh?" Diego said. "At least that's one part of the play that won't need any special effects."

"Except when Captain Hook falls into the crocodile's mouth," Bob pointed out. "You'll probably need to figure something out for that—unless you want to use a *real* crocodile."

"That might be easier than using a fake one," said Diego. "We could pick someone we really *hate* to be Captain Hook, and . . . Anyway, back to the play."

He read about the three battles and about Tinker Bell getting poisoned. Then he read the end, where Wendy and her brothers decide to return home, taking the Lost Boys with them.

"'When Wendy, John, Michael, and Nana get home, they find their parents waiting for them. They beg their parents to adopt the Lost Boys, and their parents agree. But what about Peter? At first he doesn't want to be adopted, but then he gives in and decides to move in with the Darlings after all. In the last scene of the play, we see that his flying abilities have helped him to become the most famous stunt-man in the world.'"

Diego set down the sheets of paper and smiled. "It's really good," he told Bob. "It's much, much better than mine was. You changed just the right things."

"You really think so?" Bob asked eagerly. "So you think it's okay for me to write the actual play now?"

"Sure, go ahead. How fast can you get it done?"

"Oh, it probably won't take more than a week. Bonnie's going to help me with it."

"It's great," Diego said. "Thanks a lot!"

"Oh, I almost forgot," Bob said. Reaching into his back pocket, he pulled out another sheet of paper. "Here's a list of all the special effects I think we'll need. Of course there are probably others, but these are the main ones."

"Terrific—" Diego started to say. Then he looked at what was written on the paper. "Hey, Bob!" he yelped. "This list is outrageous! What do you think? That *I* have supernatural powers or something?"

"Come on! It's not that bad," Bob said soothingly. "I didn't want to leave anything out!"

"That's one thing I don't think you need to worry about," Diego said. Then he read:

1) Make Peter fly.
2) Make Peter lose his shadow.
3) Make the kids and Nana fly. Also, make Nana. Two kids inside dog costume? Remote-control stuffed dog? Needs to be as realistic as possible.

"Maybe we can just rent some trained dog from a talent agency," Bob suggested. "And teach it not to mind being flown around the stage."

4) Flying scene in space. Need birds and talking stars.
5) Make Never-Neverland look real. Need pirates, aliens, wild animals.
6) Show Hook being helped by aliens in one fight. Need fake aliens plus alien-type special effects.
7) Show Hook changing his shape in another fight. He changes at least three times.
8) Show crocodile eating Hook. Need realistic crocodile.
9) Need realistic Tinker Bell.

"Not that stupid spotlight they sometimes use in Peter Pan plays," said Bob. "We need something that looks like a real fairy, don't you think? Something with wings."

"Oh, sure," said Diego weakly.

10) Show Peter as a grown-up doing stunts on a movie set.

Diego set the list down. "There's a lot here," he observed—a massive understatement.

"Do you think you can handle it all?" Bob asked. "Because I can always take out some of the—"

"I think I can handle it all," Diego said. "But it depends on one thing."

He stood up and walked to his bedroom door. "Mom?" he shouted down the stairs.

"Yes, dear?"

"May I please have my allowance for the next two hundred years?"

## Chapter Five

# How Not to Cast a Play

"Who *is* this girl?" Chantilly whispered to Diego. The two of them had set up chairs in front of the lunchroom stage to watch the class tryouts for the play. "I know she's in our class, but I've never heard her talk before!"

In the classroom, Sally Lou O'Donnell never raised her hand. If she had to answer a question, she spoke so faintly that you could barely hear her. But all her life, she must have been seething and bubbling with secret opinions about the theater. And trying out for *Planetary Peter Pan* had brought every single one of them out into the open.

Sally Lou stared at Diego through her big round glasses. "It doesn't make *any* sense," she said. "What about this line here, the one where

Peter says, 'You've got to give me back my shadow! I don't feel right without it!' That's a *totally* ridiculous thing to say!"

*Just read your lines if you want a part in this play!* Diego longed to yell at her. But instead, he just asked, "Why do you think that's ridiculous?"

"Because why does Peter say it to Wendy?" Sally Lou shot back. "The *dog* is the one who took the shadow. Why doesn't he say it to the dog?"

"Do you really think it makes sense for Peter to talk to a dog?" Diego replied as mildly as he could. He was doing his best not to look at Chantilly so that he wouldn't burst out laughing.

"It makes a lot more sense than what's written here!" snapped Sally Lou. "I'm not going to try out for Wendy until you make a few changes in this script!"

"That's fine, Sally Lou," Chantilly answered sweetly. "We can always use more people to be pirates or aliens. Maybe you'll be happier with a part where you don't have to say anything at all. Next!"

Diego sighed. "One down, nineteen to go," he murmured. "I thought that the hardest part of this play would be writing it. I completely forgot that we'd have to get people to play the parts."

Then he glanced around the lunchroom. It was funny how just one classroom's worth of kids could take over the whole place. Some were lined up at the edge of the stage, waiting for their turn to read. Some were leaning against the wall, muttering their lines in low voices. And some were standing off in a corner, practicing for imaginary swordfights.

Well, one person, anyway: Rocky Latizano. He was lunging back and forth, jabbing fiercely at the air and parrying invisible thrusts from his invisible opponent's invisible sword. "Now have at thee, coward!" he bellowed, making a particularly vicious sword thrust. "Hah! I've got you now!"

Then he noticed Diego was watching him and waved his invisible sword triumphantly in the air. "I just killed Peter Pan!" he shouted happily.

Chantilly looked shocked. "Rocky, the play doesn't end like—" she began.

But Diego cut her off. "Let him stay in the mood," he said. "We still haven't seen anyone who would make a good Captain Hook. Who knows? Maybe Rocky can do it. Look—he's not even eating anything. He *must* be taking this seriously!"

"Hah! I'll believe he can act when I see it," Chantilly answered. "Anyway, here comes Junior. I bet *he'll* be good at this. He's such a great salesman."

Junior strode confidently onto the stage. Diego noticed that he had loosened his tie. Maybe he thought it made him seem more casual and actor-y. "Hi, guys," he said to Diego and Chantilly. Then he snapped his fingers. "Please turn to page eleven in your scripts."

A little startled, Diego and Chantilly obeyed.

"Line three," Junior directed them. "Peter has just brought Wendy and her brothers to the planet."

Then, giving them his best businessman's smile, he began: "'ThesearetheLostBoys Tootles Slightly Nibs Curly and the Twins They willprotectyoufromthealiensandthepirates—'"

"Hold on!" Diego called. "Uh . . . could you maybe slow it down just a little, Junior? We couldn't quite understand you."

"Hey, no problem!" Junior said, glancing back at his script. "'Here'swherewe liveinthis undergroundcaveIjustfinishedwiringitwitha remote-controldevicethatletsusdetect—'"

"Junior, that's still too fast!" cried Chantilly. But it was no use. No matter how many times they told him to slow down, Junior rapidfired the words like an out-of-control jackhammer. Worse still, he didn't even seem to notice it.

At last, he was done. Snapping the script shut, he asked, "Well, that takes care of that. So what part do I get?"

Diego and Chantilly eyed each other. "We're, uh, we're not going to assign any parts until we've given everyone in the class a chance to read," Diego stammered.

"Just to be fair to everyone," Chantilly added quickly.

"Oh, I get it," Junior said. "You don't want to hurt people's feelings or anything." Then he gave them a big wink, as if to say, "We all understand that I'm talking about *other* people, don't we?" Aloud, he said, "I'll be looking forward to hearing from you." And he walked briskly off the stage.

"I can't believe him!" Chantilly grumbled. "He really thinks he did a great job! How are you going to break the news to him?"

"*Me?*" said Diego. "You mean, how are *you* going to break the news to him. That's really the director's job, don't you think?"

Chantilly was about to answer, when a voice said, "It's my turn now, isn't it?"

The speaker was Teri Beckwith. She was tall and pale, with straight black hair and a long nose. She actually looked kind of like a witch, a young glamorous witch, maybe, but still . . .

"I'd like to read for the part of Wendy Darling," Teri announced in a deep, throaty voice. Lifting her script gracefully, she shook her long black hair.

"Oh, JOHN and MICHAEL!" Teri whooped, tossing her head around like an opera singer. "What a perfectly GLORIOUS day it is. . . ."

Chantilly shook her head heavily. Diego couldn't blame her. What Teri was doing couldn't really be called reading—or acting. Probably the best description for it was *throbbing*. "A GLORIOUS, GLORIOUS DAY," Teri continued.

"Hang on a second," Diego interrupted. "I can't find any of this in my script! Where are you?"

Teri flashed him an impatient frown. "I don't have to stick with the script the whole time!" she said. "*Real* actresses always take the script and run with it. Of course, I'll need to do a little improvisation here and there to get the feeling!" And she went back to her throbbing.

"Yes, a GLORIOUS day," she trilled, "but HALT! I see something at our bedroom window!" She gasped sharply and staggered backward. "AAAAAIIIIEEEE! It's a BURGLAR!"

And she fell to the ground in a dead faint.

"Ouch!" she said in a normal voice, raising herself up on one elbow. "This floor is *hard*!"

"Well, what did you expect?" asked Chantilly sharply. "Anyway, the script doesn't say Wendy faints. She runs to get Nana!"

"Why are you being so unimaginative about this?" Teri moaned. "I'm going to get some ice for my head. And when I get back, I want us to sit down and really *talk* about this!" With that, Teri flung herself dramatically off the stage and flounced out of the lunchroom.

Diego turned to Chantilly. "We must have some very, very tiny part that would be just right for her, don't you think?" he asked.

Chantilly grinned and nodded. "Yeah, maybe she could play Nana. That's a good part for a tragedy queen."

After that, Diego and Chantilly always privately called Teri the Tragedy Queen.

Tryouts went on for another hour—a long, exhausting hour. Only two things really stood out. One was that Rocky did a great job. The second was that both Larry and Louie Watson fell off the stage while they were reading. When the last person in the class had tried out—it was Jonathan Matterhorn, and he told them right away that he was only doing it because his mother had made him—Diego hopped onto the stage.

"Could I have your attention, everyone?" he called. "You all did great jobs"—*or a couple of you did*, Diego added to himself—"and Chantilly and I will have the cast list on Mrs. Doubleday's blackboard by tomorrow morning. There will be parts for everyone," he went on quickly, wondering how he was ever going to let Junior know he wasn't going to be a star. "And, uh, of course, there will be *lots* of crowd scenes."

# Chapter Six

# Birds, Bats, and Blood

"I hate to tell you this, Diego, but you've made a big mistake," Junior said the morning after the tryouts. "You forgot to put my name on the board!"

He was staring in amazement at Mrs. Doubleday's blackboard, where, only half an hour before, Diego and Chantilly had chalked up their final choices for the cast of *Planetary Peter Pan*. And it was true that Junior Smith's name was nowhere to be seen.

Instead, Diego and Chantilly had chosen a boy named Steve Tobias to be Peter Pan. He was a wiry redhead with mischievous green eyes and pointy eyebrows. As Chantilly had told Diego while he was trying out, "He *looks* so much like Peter Pan that even if he turns

48

out to be a bad actor, it wouldn't matter too much. We could just have Bob rewrite the play. Peter Pan doesn't *have* to talk, you know." But luckily, Steve had turned out to be a good actor, too.

Bonnie Kirk was going to be Wendy, and Will Ryan and Dan Munter were going to be John and Michael. Since John and Michael didn't have much to say, Diego and Chantilly had simply picked the two guys in the class who looked the most like Bonnie. Rocky was Captain Hook, to everyone's surprise—including his own.

The less important parts—Mr. and Mrs. Darling, the Lost Boys, and a couple of other characters like Smee and Tiger Lily—had all been filled. But Diego and Chantilly hadn't been able to decide who would play the all-important role of Nana the dog.

Chantilly had totally vetoed Bob's idea of renting a trained dog. "It's going to be bad enough directing the Watson twins without throwing a dog in!" she exploded. "Now, if you wanted to *replace* Louie and Larry with a trained dog, that would be okay," she added thoughtfully.

As he stared into Junior's confused face, Diego had an idea. *Who knows*, he thought,

*Junior might be perfect for the part of Nana! But I'd better not get his hopes up....*

"Actually, Junior," he said slowly, "we didn't forget to put your name up there. Lots of people read well, but there just weren't enough parts to go around. I'm sorry."

Junior's face fell. "Oh," he said.

"But actually," Diego continued. "A play's not that great a business opportunity, if you think about it."

Junior brightened immediately. "You know," he said. "I never thought about that! But you're absolutely right! In fact, being in a play might really *hurt* my career! Like, say I forget just one line and all the rich business-men in the audience think, 'Well, I'm certainly never going to hire *that* loser!' Why, that would be a real tragedy."

"It sure would," Diego said heartily.

"Besides," Junior went on, "I can probably do more for the play by working behind the scenes, if you know what I mean.... For example, take a look at this." He pushed a piece of paper into Diego's hand.

Diego looked it over. It was a list of names. Some of them sounded familiar, but Diego couldn't think why.

"What is this?" he asked.

50

"It's the names of the hundred richest people in Pasadena," Junior told him proudly.

Now Diego realized why he thought he recognized some of the names. He had heard them on the local news, or read about them in the papers. . . . Alicia Wu was a college girl who had inherited a huge chain of grocery stores. Gregory Dean was a horse breeder. Adam Poulios was the owner of the Pasadena Earthquakes, the only football team in the entire world that had never won a single game. . . .

"How did you put this list together?" he asked Junior.

"Oh, you know, I just did it," Junior replied vaguely. "The thing is, I bet we can get money for the special effects for our play from some of these guys. In fact, I'm planning to start tracking them down on Saturday. Want to come along?"

"Sure," Diego said.

It wasn't his idea of a great way to spend a Saturday. But Diego couldn't help thinking that if he *didn't* come along, any money Junior collected would never make it into *Planetary Peter Pan*. It would stay right in Junior's pockets. . . .

"Of course I'd love to help you fellas," Mr. Chet Richards rumbled. He was the first person on Junior's list. Taking a deep puff of his smelly cigar, Mr. Richards leaned back in his comfortable leather-cushioned chair. "I like to see kids who want to get ahead. It's never too early to start trying to make money, that's what I say." And he looked around approvingly at his black leather and gold trimmed office.

"We're not exactly trying to make money for ourselves," Diego reminded him in a strangled voice. He was trying not to cough from the cigar smoke Mr. Richards kept blowing into his face. "It's for the play our class is doing."

"Yes, yes. . . . Anyway, fellows, I'm going to help you out. You're an enterprising pair, and I admire that!"

"Oh, that's wonderful of you, sir," gushed Junior.

"Think nothing of it." Mr. Richards heaved a sigh and flopped around in his chair until he managed to pull his wallet out of his pocket. "I wish you the best of luck. Here you go. No, don't bother thanking me. I *like* helping people."

And into Junior's eager hand he placed a single dollar bill.

Junior and Diego had no better luck at the next two places they tried. The first was the huge house of an elderly woman named Margaret Lawrence. Mrs. Lawrence was busy giving her huge St. Bernard a bath in the back when Junior and Diego walked up.

"Certainly, dear," Mrs. Lawrence said vaguely when Junior had finished his prepared speech. "I'll be happy to—Trinket, stop wiggling!—I'll be happy to give you two thousand dollars!" She stopped washing the dog and peered round. "It's in my purse over there— oh, no it isn't. Trinket, cut it out! Now, where did I leave my money? I went to the bank just the other—Trinket, *no!*—You'd better give me your address so I can mail it to you. North Central High School, isn't that what you said? Trinket! Hold still!"

"Two thousand dollars! Wow!" said Junior as they left Mrs. Lawrence's house. "That should be enough, don't you think?"

"Sure," Diego said glumly, "if we ever see the money." He couldn't help thinking that Mrs. Lawrence had been so wrapped up in giving Trinket a bath that she hadn't really heard a word they'd said.

Another little old lady was next on their list. Her problem was that she thought they shouldn't *need* any special effects. "It's a charming story just the way it is! Anyway, in my day, children had imagination! When they wanted to fly, they just shut their eyes and pretended." She closed her eyes tight and gave a funny little hop in the air to demonstrate. "That's how it should be," she said firmly.

And six rich people later, the only money Junior and Diego had collected was Mr. Richards's dollar. "I've had it," Diego said grouchily as they left the office of their ninth rich person. "This is ridiculous. If you want to keep on trying, go ahead. I'm going home."

But Junior was still in a good mood. "A good businessman never gives up," he said breezily. "I'll try a few more places. I know one of them will be happy to sponsor us. And who knows, maybe someone will remember how enterprising I was and offer me a job someday!"

No money meant no special effects. And it was horrible having to rehearse *Planetary Peter Pan* without knowing exactly what the special effects were going to be. Diego kept trying to stall, but everybody connected with the play was starting to get just a little impatient.

"Okay, Steve, now Peter jumps out of Nana's way!" Chantilly called to Steve Tobias during one afternoon rehearsal.

Up on stage, Steve started to jump, then stopped in his tracks. "But where is Nana supposed to be standing?" he asked.

"Oh, in back of you somewhere," Chantilly

told him. "Now, make sure you look scared. Remember, she's trying to bite your shadow off!"

"Give me a break!" protested Steve. "I can't look scared of something that's not there! I don't have that good an imagination! When are we going to have a *real* Nana?"

Chantilly turned to Diego, who was standing next to her watching the rehearsal. "Well?" she asked crossly.

Diego shrugged. "I don't know yet."

"Come on, Diego. You *have* to know!" Chantilly burst out. "We can't just keep faking it like this."

"Yeah," said Steve indignantly. "It's totally lame."

Diego looked at the ground. "Well..." he began.

"Look," Chantilly said, "can't you make a dog out of papier-mâché or something?"

"That would be totally stupid!" Diego snapped.

"Don't you think it's totally stupid that we're three weeks away from opening night and we still don't know what kind of weapons we're going to use or what kind of aliens are on the planet or even what kind of dog we're—"

"Okay, okay!" Diego sighed. "Give me one more weekend. If I can't come up with something by Monday, I'll get out the construction paper and spray paint.... I promise."

That happened on Friday. Late Saturday afternoon, Diego climbed onto his bike and set out for the nearest art-supply store to buy construction paper and spray paint. He hadn't completely given up, but there was no sense in leaving things until Sunday, when none of the stores would be open.

He had almost reached the mall when he passed his favorite store. It was called Toys of the Future.

Toys of the Future was more than a toy store. It looked like some gleaming outpost of an empire from a thousand years in the future. And there weren't toys in there—at least not toys like dolls or games. Instead, there were what was called "entertainment inventions," usually things that had to be seen to be believed.

Diego checked his watch. He had half an hour before the art store closed....

And half an hour later, Diego was still inside Toys of the Future. He was playing with one of the neatest toys he had ever seen, an eight-hundred-dollar, one-quarter-size, remote-controlled Porsche that could climb walls and even drive upside down across the ceiling.

"These are great, aren't they?" asked someone next to him.

Diego turned to see a young brown-haired man in jeans and a leather jacket standing next to him. "They're fantastic," he agreed. "But I still can't understand how they go across the ceiling like that!"

"It's actually pretty simple," the man said. "There's a sensor in the motor that tells the car when its upside down. As soon as the sensor switches on, the car begins to generate a current that bonds it to the ceiling—kind of like static electricity. But you can't pause for even a fraction of a second before the car gets to the ceiling, or it will fall."

"Wow! How do you know all this?" Diego asked.

The man smiled. "I invented the car."

"What do you mean? Are you a toy person or something?"

"No, actually I'm a movie person. I only design toys once in a while. Mostly I do special effects for movies. Do you know what special effects are?"

"Do I know what they *are*?" Diego blurted out. "They're all I think about these days! Have you worked on any movies I might have heard of?"

The man looked a little uncomfortable. "Well, yes, actually. I mean, I assume you've heard of *Silverworld*. It was kind of a big deal a couple years ago."

"*Silverworld!*" Diego gasped. "Of course I've heard of it! I've seen it fifteen times! You mean, you did the special effects for *that*?"

"Uh-huh," the man said awkwardly.

"I can't believe it! What's your name?"

"Tom Glade."

"And what are you doing here in Pasadena? Don't you live in some giant mansion in Beverly Hills or something?"

Tom grinned. "Well, yes, I do, as a matter of fact. But I've got a studio here in town, too. I just wanted to come by Toys of the Future and see how— Why are you looking at me like that?"

Diego took a deep breath. "Tom, you're not going to believe this, but—but I think my guardian angel sent you to find me."

Diego never did get that construction paper. Once he'd explained his Peter Pan problem, what he got instead was an invitation to visit Tom's studio the next day and see if there was anything there he could use in the play. By eleven o'clock Sunday morning, Diego and his father were on their way.

"Here we are," Mr. Lopez said as they pulled up to a low-lying white building on Papagallo Road. A small sign over the front door said

"Glade Creations." "Do you want me to come in with you?" he asked Diego. He looked longingly at the newspaper on the front seat next to him.

"No, that's okay," Diego said. "I won't be gone long."

The minute he opened the front door to Tom's studio, Diego knew something was wrong. Of course, it doesn't take you long to realize something's wrong when you open a front door and step into a pool of blood.

Horrified, Diego peered into the gloom around him. He was in a vast, cavernous room. And a trail of bloody footprints was leading away from the front door and across the room into . . . into what?

"Tom!" he croaked fearfully. "Is everything al—"

With a terrifying shriek, a huge black bird swooped down on him, talons outstretched. Diego ducked just in time. Cackling fiendishly, the bird swooped back up toward the ceiling.

"I've got to get out of here!" Diego thought in a panic. He turned and fumbled blindly with the door handle. But the second he touched it, all the lights went out. And then he realized the door was locked!

That's when Diego heard the maniacal laughter from the next room.

"A-HAH-HAH-HAH-HAH-HAH-HAH—"
*Click!*

As abruptly as it had begun, the laughter switched off.

"A-HAH-HAH-HAH-HAH-HAH-HAH—"
*Click!*

"Darn it!" Diego heard someone complain in the next room. "That's not right! Where's the..."

"Tom?" Diego quavered. "Is that you?"

"Diego? Is that *you*? What time is it?"

And, to Diego's astonishment, Tom came strolling into the front hallway as if nothing was wrong.

"It's not eleven yet, is it?" he asked.

"Y-yes, it is!" Diego stammered. "Hey, are you—are you all right?"

"All right?" Tom repeated. "What are you talking about?"

"Well, the blood...and that bird...I thought you'd been killed or something!"

"The bird!" Tom gasped. "I forgot to turn off the bird! Oh, gosh, I'm really sorry. You must have been a little startled!"

He reached over to the wall and flipped a switch. "The raven's motion-activated," he explained. "When the front door opens, it waits a few seconds and then dives."

"You mean it's not real?"

"No, no." Tom laughed. "I built it a few years ago. Kind of a security system, you might say. I meant to make sure to turn it off before you got here, but I forgot." He smiled ruefully. "Some welcome, huh?"

"And the b-b-blood?" Diego stammered.

"Fake. Just a little decoration. My friends say I have a sick sense of humor. I guess they're right."

Tom flipped another switch on the wall, and the room sprang into light. "Anyway, come in and look around," he said.

Diego peered up at the ceiling. The mechanical bird was crouched up on a metal beam waiting for its next victim. Diego could see what looked like dozens of bats up there, too.

"Are *they* fake, too?" he said.

"Yup. Sound-activated. Watch this." Tom clapped his hands sharply three times. The bats flew down from the ceiling in a fluttering cloud, circled the room, and returned to the beam again.

Then Diego noticed that the room they were standing in was lined with bookshelves. But instead of holding books, the shelves were filled with all kinds of strange objects. "What is all this stuff?" he asked.

"Just take a look," Tom said.

There were blood capsules that you hid in

your pockets and pressed when you wanted to look wounded. There were spray cans filled with neon-colored dyes that disappeared thirty seconds after you'd sprayed them on. There were about a hundred different kinds of false teeth that fitted over your own teeth so you could look like Dracula or Metal Mouth or a sharp-toothed alien. There were fake icicles filled with real water so that they could drip without melting. There were swords where you pressed the handle, and a beam of colored light jumped out into the air like a laser.

"Don't forget to look into my zoo," Tom said after a while. He opened the door to another huge room that looked exactly like a jungle. A carpet of tall, thick grass lay on the floor, and the walls were painted with strange, gnarled trees. Standing frozen in the grass were a gorilla, a wolf, a mastodon, a saber-toothed tiger, and all kinds of other animals. They were all life-sized, and unbelievably life-like.

"Amazing," Diego gasped.

"They're remote-controlled," Tom said. "I devised a keyboard to operate them. It's a lot easier than punching buttons."

"Hey, maybe we could do Nana that way!" said Diego.

"I don't see why not," Tom answered. "But

you might rather use a person in a costume. You get more range of motion. I've got some incredible costumes in the next room, if you're interested."

"You've got some incredible *everything*!" Diego raved. "I can't believe this! And it's really okay for us to borrow it?"

"Of course it is," Tom replied. "But it sounds as though you'll have to create lots of effects for your play that even I don't have, but I can show you how to make them. And you're always welcome to my tools and my books."

"Fantastic!" Diego exclaimed.

## Chapter Seven

# Rule Number One:
# Avoid Rehearsals

"Could you pull the platform a little higher?" called Diego from his spot at the edge of the stage.

"I'll try," Bob puffed. He tugged the pulley that was hoisting a six-foot wooden platform loaded with machinery up the wall at the back of the stage. "Wow, this is heavy!" he exclaimed. "What is it, exactly?"

"It's one of our aliens," Diego replied. "Or its insides, anyway. I'll make the outside later. See, the alien's going to be mounted on the wall up there, and it will swivel back and forth during the fight scenes!"

"Does it shoot?" Bob asked, fastening the pulley rope around its hook. "Or does it just swing back and forth like a gigantic hula dancer?"

"Of course it shoots!" Diego said. "It shoots huge beams of light that vaporize anyone they touch. We're using liquid nitrogen for the vaporizing part."

"Sounds good," said Bob. "I hope it gets me. I'd love to see my sister's reaction when I get vaporized onstage."

"Oh, she'll have a fit," Diego promised him. "It's totally realistic. Knowing your sister, she'll probably want to jump onstage and try it herself."

Ever since Diego had visited Tom's studio, the play had been sailing along perfectly. Diego had borrowed dozens of special effects and learned how to make lots more. *Planetary Peter Pan*'s Never-Neverland was going to have three different kinds of aliens now, and in Diego's opinion they were all pretty awesome. The flying in the play was going to look totally realistic, too, as long as the actors who were flying didn't panic as they zoomed through the air on their invisible wires. And the crocodile that swallowed Captain Hook at the end of the play looked so natural that even Diego felt a little nervous every time it opened its jaws.

Before Tom had supplied him with all this

stuff, Diego had dreaded coming to rehearsals. Now he actually enjoyed them.

Diego stepped back from the stage and stared happily at all the activity going on around him. One group of kids was starting to put together the set that Tiffany had designed. Another group was painting a backdrop for the scene where Peter and the Darlings flew to Never-Neverland. And a few of the main characters in the play were sitting around a lunch table going over their lines. (Chantilly had let the kids playing secondary characters stay at home, for once.)

The play was only two weeks away, but amazingly enough, everything seemed to be going smoothly. . . .

"Now that we've got the alien up there, what's next?" Bob asked.

"Let's see," Diego said. "I guess we should start working on the—"

"Diego, can I talk to you for a minute?"

It was Jennifer Stevens. "I've got the finished costume sketches to show you," she said. She plunked a lavender leather portfolio down on the edge of the stage.

"Great!" said Diego. *Uh-oh*, he thought. *Just when things were starting to go well!* "Is Chantilly around?" he asked, hoping to stall for a few seconds. "I'd like her to see them, too."

"I'll go get her," said Jennifer.

Chantilly had been coaching Rocky in one corner of the lunchroom. She looked completely exhausted as she came walking over to Diego.

"Having trouble?" Diego asked.

"He's impossible," Chantilly said briefly. "I don't want to talk about it right now. Let's see your sketches, Jennifer!"

Jennifer untied the ribbon holding the portfolio closed and pulled out a stack of sketches.

"I took your advice, Diego," she said proudly. She spread the sketches out along the edge of the stage. "These costumes are just what you wanted. Very high-tech. Very streamlined. Well? What do you think?"

It was certainly true that Jennifer had made one improvement from her original concept: Peter Pan wasn't wearing a leaf skirt anymore. But was the spangled blue outfit he was wearing now really *that* much an improvement? To Diego, it looked as though all Peter needed was a pair of skates and he'd be able to join the Ice Capades.

And the dress Jennifer had designed for Wendy was like something a fairy-tale princess would wear—if she wanted to belt out a song in Las Vegas, that is. But the real shocker was Captain Hook's costume. Gone were the long black curls, the pirate's patch, the three-cornered pirate's hat, the red jacket, and the sword. In their place was a lovely one-piece number that looked more than anything like—

"A *jumpsuit!*" howled Diego, and he burst into a fit of laughter. "Why is Captain Hook in a jumpsuit?"

"It's not a jumpsuit," Jennifer replied stiffly. "It's a one-piece fighting outfit. Orange is a violent color." Her lip wobbled. "Anyway," she burst out, "you said to make the costumes more up-to-date!"

Chantilly rushed in to soothe Jennifer's ruffled feelings. "And they certainly are *very* up-to-date, Jennifer," she said, "but what I think Diego means is that it not very...pirate-y. Isn't that what you mean, Diego?"

She gave Diego a pleading glance. *Try to get a hold of yourself!* she seemed to be saying.

Diego struggled to control himself. "Th-that's right," he choked out, biting the insides of his cheeks to calm himself down. "It's more like something a—well—a, a space pumpkin would wear. And where's his hook?"

"Oh, I don't want him to have a hook," Jennifer said. "It's much too gross, don't you think?"

"Jennifer, he's got to have a hook," Diego

said flatly. "And what kind of pirate hat is *that*?" It was big and bright orange, and it looked more like a bowl covered with feathers than anything else. "That hat," said Diego, "has *got* to go!"

"Well!" Jennifer snapped, glaring at Diego. "I suppose you want everyone to be dressed in aluminum foil with hooks on *everything*!" And she grabbed the sketches and stuffed them into her portfolio.

"Wait a second!" Diego cried. "Let me see the rest of your—"

"Forget it!" sniffed Jennifer. She retied the portfolio and gave the bow a vicious tug. "Why should I show them to *you*? Just so you can laugh at me? No way! Not until I've done them all over again just to make you happy. It will take me forever, but *you* probably don't care about that!" And she marched off across the lunchroom.

"Well, Diego," Chantilly said when Jennifer was gone, "that was very, very smooth. It was bad enough when she kept interrupting rehearsals so she could measure people. Now she'll start measuring them again, *and* sulk while she's doing it!"

"I'm sorry," Diego said. "I really am. I don't know what got into me."

"Well, if you're that sorry, come and talk to

Rocky with me," Chantilly said. "He's being just horrible."

"What do you mean?" Diego asked. "I thought he was a good actor!"

Chantilly sighed. "He *is* a good actor," she told him. "But he's *not* a good memorizer. Come with me, and you'll see what I mean."

Rocky was still in the corner of the lunch-room where Chantilly had left him. He was bent studiously over his script, muttering to himself. At his feet were two crumpled-up giant-size bags of barbecue-flavor potato chips, six cans of soda, and four candy bars.

"Hey, Rock," Diego said. "How's it going?"

"Great!" Rocky looked up, beaming. "I've really got this down now, Chantilly. Try me!"

"Rocky, that's fantastic!" Chantilly said, looking surprised. "I never thought you'd be able to do it! Let's hear a few of your lines!" She opened her copy of the script.

Rocky hooked his thumbs into his belt, rocked back and forth on his heels, and began in a loud, confident voice, " 'Today's the day, my hearties. I feel it in my bones. Today's the day we'll nab Peter Pan and...' "

He paused. " 'And... we'll...' "

" 'We'll finally rid the planet of...' " Chantilly prompted.

" 'And we'll finally rid the planet of that . . .' "

"It begins with *l*," Chantilly reminded him.

" 'Of that l-l'—Let's see, it's something about Peter, right?"

"Right," Chantilly agreed grimly.

"And it begins with *l*. Lunch. Lady. Lion. Leopard. London. Just give me a little hint, Chantilly, okay?"

"Okay. 'And we'll finally rid the planet of that lily- . . .' "

"Lily! That's right! 'And we'll finally rid the planet of that lily lunch!' "

*"Lily lunch?"* said Chantilly incredulously. "What are you talking about? The line is, 'And we'll finally rid the planet of that lily-livered coward!' "

"Oh," said Rocky. "Well, liver, lunch, it's all food, right? Hey, look, I was *close*, anyway."

"You were *not* close!" Chantilly shrieked. She turned to Diego. "Do you see what this is like? *You* try making him realize that he's got to memorize his lines!"

Diego put his hand on Chantilly's shoulder. "Rocky," he began in his calmest, most soothing voice. "We've only got two more weeks, right? And if you don't learn your lines, Rocky, we'll all look bad. Now, it's not that hard. You've just got to make yourself sit down and go over and over the lines. That's the only way to learn them."

Rocky shrugged. "I just *can't*," he said cheerfully. "It's impossible. I tried, and I just can't do it."

"So what are you planning to do on the night of the play?" Diego asked in amazement.

"Oh, I'm sure I'll know them by then. Probably."

"But Rocky," Diego began, "that's a—"

"Hello, everyone!" came a booming voice behind him. "How goes our little drama?"

Diego didn't even have to turn around to see who it was. "Oh, brother," he muttered. "Mr. Haypence. That's *all* we need."

From the look of it, Mr. Haypence planned to spend a good long time at today's rehearsal. He strode briskly into the lunchroom, sat down at one of the tables, leaned back, and took out a little notebook.

"Let's see it from the top!" he called out, pencil poised to take notes.

Diego and Chantilly exchanged nervous glances. "We're not really rehearsing this afternoon, Mr. Haypence," Chantilly said after a long pause. "Not a full-scale rehearsal, that is. We'll be having a real rehearsal tomorrow, though, if you'd like to come back then," she added hopefully.

"No, no, that won't do. They'll be putting tile around the new pool, and I'm sure they'll need my input. Well, if I can't see a real rehearsal, how about just showing me a scene or two? Where is"—he permitted himself a hearty chuckle—"Mr. Pan?"

Steve and Bonnie were going over their lines together across the room. "Uh, Steve?" Diego called. "Could you come over here a second? I've got a little surprise for you."

The look on Steve's face made it clear that he knew what the little surprise was. He walked slowly across the floor, dragging his feet every step of the way. "Hello, Mr. Haypence," he mumbled, staring at the floor.

"Hello, *Peter*!" boomed Mr. Haypence. "Well, young man, let's see you fly."

"Fly?" echoed Steve.

"I presume that in this production, Peter *does* fly?" Mr. Haypence said.

*Has Mr. Haypence finally gone over the edge?* Diego wondered.

"He doesn't actually *fly*, Mr. Haypence," Diego explained. "We do it with wires hung from the ceiling. See, I've been talking to this special-effects guy who's been—"

"Wires!" Mr. Haypence looked indignant. "What rubbish! You don't need to do it with *wires*!" he puffed. "That's not the art of stage-

74

craft. No, what a real actor does is create the *illusion* of flight by skillful body motions! Here, allow me to demonstrate. As you may know, I've starred in many a school play myself."

As Diego, Chantilly, Rocky, and Steve goggled at him, Mr. Haypence climbed heavily onto a lunch chair and stretched out his arms, frowning with concentration. Then he began dipping and swaying back and forth like an enormous, clumsy mechanical bear.

"You see how real that looks?" he asked as he lurched from side to side. "With just a few movements, I have you completely convinced that I'm actually soaring through the air!"

"But Mr. Haypence, you *don't* have me completely—" began Rocky. Mr. Haypence didn't seem to hear him, though.

"And add a few hops, and I seem almost weightless!" he said. Just then, his foot went crashing through the bottom of the chair, and down he went like a very *heavy* mechanical bear.

"Ouch," he yelped. "Just a little accident. I— Ouch!"

## Chapter Eight

# Limping Toward Stardom

"Stay, Trinket! Stay!" Diego commanded. "Don't you even *think* about that hamster cage!"

"How much longer do I have to stand around in this stupid costume?" came Junior's muffled voice from behind the dog mask he was wearing. "It's been two hours already!"

"Where do you want me to install this motor again, Diego?" asked Bob.

"Not much longer, Junior. It's only been *half* an hour," Diego said. "Try putting it behind the dog's ear," he said to Bob. "The ear of the dog *mask*, I mean. Not the real dog's ear."

Every inch of Diego's floor was covered—you might say carpeted—with special effects he and Bob had been working on. The only clear spots were right underfoot—right under *feet*, to be exact.

At the moment, there were twelve feet in the room. Two weren't alive. They belonged to a full-sized model of an alien that was going to be used in the background of one of Peter Pan and Captain Hook's big fight scenes. And four of the living feet belonged to Trinket. Trinket was the massive St. Bernard who belonged to Mrs. Lawrence, the distracted dog-washer Diego and Junior had asked for money before Tom Glade had come along. When he'd started working on the mask for Nana, Diego had suddenly remembered Trinket. He'd called Mrs. Lawrence, and she'd agreed to let them use her St. Bernard as a model.

It wasn't too much trouble having Trinket in the room. She was as peaceful—and almost as big—as a cow. Her only fault seemed to be that she was much too interested in the rows of cages along Diego's wall.

Two more (also living) feet belonged to Junior, who was standing in the middle of the room in his dog costume. "This is awful," he whined. "I won't put up with this much longer, you know!"

"It won't *be* much longer," Diego promised. "Now hold still, Junior. Bob's got to install this little motor in your ear—I mean, in Nana's ear. And then I'll finish painting the head."

Junior was going to be dressed in a dog costume made of plush. That part was pretty ordinary. It was the dog-head mask he would be wearing that was impressive. With Tom's help, Diego had managed to make a latex St. Bernard's head that looked exactly like the real thing. And the tiny motor concealed inside one of the mask's ears was going to make Nana's mouth open and close just like a real dog's. Of course, someone offstage would have to play a tape during the times when Nana was supposed to be barking. (When Junior had tried to bark, it had come out as a squawk instead.) But Diego was sure it would go smoothly.

Now all that was left to do was install the motor, paint the mask, and, last but not least, teach Junior how to act like a St. Bernard.

"Okay, Junior. Hold still for a second," Diego directed. "I'm painting the nose now. And while I'm doing that, why don't you watch Trinket so you can pick up some tips?"

"What *kind* of tips?" yelped Junior. "She's just standing there!"

"I know, but she's paying attention to everything. And that's just how Nana should act. See the way Trinket sniffs the air as if she's looking for food? In Never-Neverland, Nana would probably—*Trinket!* Stay!"

But it was too late. Trinket was already lunging across the room toward the row of cages. And as she went, her big, heavy feet crushed dozens of the tiny, fragile special-effects things Diego had been working on.

"Bob, stop her!" Diego cried frantically. "My hands are covered with paint!"

"I—I can't!" Bob said helplessly. "I'm afraid I'll step on something, too!"

As they watched, paralyzed, Trinket leapt up to the hamster cage and sniffed it curiously. Then, to Diego's intense relief, she turned away and began to crunch slowly across the floor again.

"Good dog," said Diego sincerely. "*Good* dog—No! No! Trinket, *don't*—"

But once again, it was too late. The words "good dog" had started Trinket wagging her tail. And her tail, just as oversized as the rest of her, wagged right into the full-sized model of the alien. The alien crashed to the floor, where it shattered instantly into a pile of plastic shards.

"You want me to act like *her*?" asked Junior incredulously. "I can't believe it!"

* * *

"Well, we finally cleaned everything up," Diego told Chantilly in school that Monday as they walked to lunch together. "Then I got my mom to drive Trinket home before she did any more damage. I don't know what's going to happen with the alien. We may have to bag it."

"Where should we sit?" he asked her when they'd gotten their trays.

She sighed. "With Rocky, I guess. He's trying to work out some kind of system for memorizing his lines."

"Well, at least he's worked out a system for eating his lunch while he's memorizing his lines," commented Diego as they walked over to Rocky. "Are you sure sitting with him won't ruin your appetite?"

Rocky's face was bent studiously toward a huge, crumpled pile of papers. And he was cramming stew into his mouth with his bare hands.

"Huh, guyve," he greeted them. He swallowed. "I mean, hi, guys. Sorry about the no-fork stuff. When I'm reading, it's hard for me to get a fork into my mouth every time—so I just decided to give up."

"Rocky, you're the *worst*," Diego said affectionately. "It's lucky I've been around you so long, or you'd make me sick. By the way, I hear you've got a system for memorizing your lines."

"Oh, yeah! It's great!" said Rocky. "Here, take a look!" He grabbed a crumpled, grimy sheet of paper and held it out. "You don't mind if I eat while you read, do you?"

"Not at all. Go ahead and get it out of the way before I have to look at you again," Diego said.

Now he realized that Rocky's "system" was scribbled onto a napkin. He read:

PETER PAN = PEANUT BUTTER

WENDY = WATERMELON

CAPTAIN HOOK = COOKED HAM

TINKER BELL = TUNA MELT

PIRATES = PIES

That's as far as Diego got. "Rocky, what *is* this?" he asked in astonishment.

Rocky wiped his mouth on his sleeve. "It's simple!" he said. "See, I can't remember lines, but I can remember *food*. So, say I have a line like, 'Ahoy! I spy Peter Pan!' Well, no one could remember something hard like that. But if I think of it as 'Ahoy! I spy peanut butter!'—well, then I don't have any trouble."

"Give me another example," Diego said slowly. He leafed through Rocky's script for a second. "Here, take this line on page twelve. 'I'll rend him from limb to limb.' How would you remember *that*?"

"Well, I haven't worked out the whole system yet, but . . . let's see. I guess that line would be 'I'll roast him from lamb to lamb.' Wait a minute. Why are you banging your head on the table like that?"

"I'm just congratulating myself," Diego said.

"For what?" asked Rocky suspiciously.

"For how very, very well-prepared we all are for this play. *And* for getting us all into this."

"Cool," Rocky said, cramming the last of his stew into his mouth. "But that's a weird way of congratulating yourself, if you ask me."

## Chapter Nine

# Dress-rehearsal Disaster

"Okay, guys," said Chantilly. She was standing next to Diego on the stage in the lunchroom, looking down at the rest of the class. She held up her hand for silence. "This is it."

"*What* is it?" asked Jonathan Matterhorn.

"*This* is! This dress rehearsal!" answered Chantilly.

"Oh, that! You were holding up your hand, so I thought you were talking about your ring or something."

"Well, I wasn't," Chantilly said a little crossly. "I meant that this is our last chance to get everything perfect for tomorrow night. We'll wear our costumes. We'll say our lines perfectly, and that means you, Rocky." She jumped off the stage and clapped her hands. "Places, everyone!"

Diego walked to the wings and slowly pulled back the electric-blue velvet curtain. A spotlight shone on a little white house somewhere in Pasadena—the Darlings' house. Wendy, John, and Michael Darling stepped out of the wings, and the play began.

For the first thirty seconds, the play went perfectly. Then Wendy's dress fell off.

Luckily, Bonnie Kirk—who was, of course, inside the dress—grabbed it back up before anyone had realized what was going on. Not that Bonnie felt like keeping what had just happened to her a secret. "Where's Jennifer?" she yelled at the top of her lungs.

"I'm backstage," Jennifer's voice floated out. "What's your problem?"

"Jennifer, it's *your* problem! What did you sew this with, fairy thread?"

Bonnie was struggling to hold the dress up around her as she spoke, but it wasn't easy. "I'll help!" called Tiffany from the wings. She rushed up and threw herself protectively in front of Bonnie.

"Hey, I know how to sew!" Jennifer protested. "I used, like, real thread and stuff! Just because *some* people go throwing themselves all over the stage instead of walking like a normal person—"

Bonnie had to keep bobbing her head up and down to get past Tiffany, who was guarding her like a basketball player. "I *wasn't* throwing myself around!" she yelled. "I took ten steps in this dress, and—"

"Okay, okay," Chantilly said quickly from her chair in the front row. "Bonnie, why don't you run backstage and change into your regular clothes? Jennifer, you can restitch the dress tonight. Now, let's start over. Places, everyone!"

There were no major problems with the other costumes after that—except that Michael Darling's pants split, and Peter Pan's tunic was so long that it looked like a dress and he kept tripping over it, and the feathers drifted, one by one, off of Tiger Lily's headdress, and one of the aliens' heads had been sewed onto the shoulders backward. Other than that, the costumes were perfect, except for the way Captain Hook's scabbard kept popping undone and the way Mrs. Darling's sleeves were so tight that her arms couldn't squeeze into them, and the way...

At last, Chantilly called a halt. Her voice was calm, but you could tell she was a little upset. "Jennifer, these costumes are a real disappointment," she said. "There's no other word for it."

"Hey, I'm sorry!" Jennifer snapped huffily. "It's not as though costumes are the only thing I spend my time on, you know."

"Well, they should have been," Chantilly told her sternly, "this week, anyway. Now, I want everybody to change back into regular clothes. And Jennifer, I want you to take all these home and fix them." She gave a weary sigh and checked her watch. "After that, we'll start over."

There were no more costume troubles after that. Instead, there were Rocky troubles—and they started with Rocky's first lines.

"'Ahoy, fellow pies!'" he bellowed lustily. "'I spy Peanut Butter and Tuna Melt! They'll not escape this time. No, I'll catch that little scallion and roast him from lamb to lamb, or my name's not Cooked Ham!'"

He stopped. Everyone was staring at him.

"Well, go on," he said to Rob Farmen, who was playing Smee. "It's your line!"

"Wait a sec," said Chantilly. There was an ominous expression on her face. "Rocky, could we please hear *your* lines again?"

"Sure," Rocky said confidently. "I've everything down cold. 'Ahoy, fellow pies! I spy a french fry alien—'"

He got no farther. Chantilly cut him off. And this time her voice was *not* calm.

"I knew it!" she shrieked. She stormed up to him and grabbed him by the shoulders. Diego heard Tiffany give a little gasp of fright from the wings. "You and your stupid system!" Chantilly fumed. "You memorized those stupid names you made up instead of the real words! You said Cooked Ham instead of the real words! You said Tuna Melt instead of Tinker Bell! You said scallion instead of *rap*-scallion! You—"

"Hey, loosen up!" Rocky protested. He tried to slide down out of Chantilly's grip, but she wouldn't let him. "Listen, I—"

Once again, Chantilly interrupted. "No, you listen to *me*." Her voice was tight with fury. "You are going to learn that part. And you're going to learn it *right*. And if you don't know every word by heart tomorrow night, I will— I will *personally* see to it that you never taste a cheeseburger in this lunchroom again!"

Diego hadn't seen Chantilly so mad since her first day at school. Now she let go of Rocky and stomped off the stage and picked up a copy of the script. "You can read from this for the rest of the rehearsal," she commanded Rocky. "And I don't want to hear another word out of you until you really, really *know* your lines."

She paused for breath and then went on. "Okay. We're starting over for the *last* time. And if anyone forgets even one word, I'll roast him from limb to limb."

"Boy, talk about pushy directors!" said Rocky with a weak laugh. But no one chimed in.

There were no more troubles after that. Everyone was too scared that Chantilly would fly into another rage. Instead, there were set troubles.

The problem wasn't with the actual sets. Tiffany had done a fine job with them.

No, the problem was with Larry Watson. And it happened during one of the fight scenes, when he died just a little too realistically.

"AAAAAAAAAAAAAAHHHHHH! THEY GOT ME!" he screamed at the top of his lungs, and hurled himself into the air. He hit the ground with a horrible *whump* and lay there, writhing in agony, for several seconds.

"Hey, he's a better actor than I thought!" Diego said to himself.

Then, coughing horribly, Larry dragged himself to his feet, picked up his sword, waved it weakly in the air, staggered backward, and knocked down one of the painted cardboard walls behind him.

"Oops," he said. "Sorry."

"My set! My set!" Tiffany wailed. She dashed out of the wings and grabbed frantically at the edge of the collapsed wall. "It's *ruined*!" She tried desperately to prop the wall up against the others, but it kept sliding down.

Suddenly, Larry smacked himself in the side of the head. "I'm such a doof!" he said. "What am I just standing around for? Here, let me give you a hand."

"*No!*" Chantilly called out. But it was too late. Larry gave the wall a nice, strong push— so nice and strong that the entire wall folded in half.

"Oops," he said again. "Sorry."

Before Tiffany could say anything, Chantilly jumped up onto the stage. "Okay, you guys. Rehearsal's over," she said quietly.

Everyone stared at her. "What do you mean?" yelled Junior, pushing back his Nana mask. "We're not even halfway done!"

"We're *done*," Chantilly said firmly. "There's no point in doing any more tonight."

Diego strode out of the wings. "Chantilly is right," he said. "We've done enough for one night. Anyway," he added to himself, "it's time to bury this disaster." He turned to Tiffany. "Do you need any help making a new wall? I'd be glad to give you a hand."

To his surprise, Tiffany shook her head. "I can handle it," she said in a slightly quavery voice. "I have more cardboard at home, and my parents can help me if I need it. I'll have my dad drive me to school early tomorrow so I can put the wall back up."

Diego looked at her with surprise. *I guess Tiffany doesn't fall apart when there's a real crisis,* he thought. "Okay, then," he said. "Let's clean up and get out of here."

From the quiet way everyone filed out of the lunchroom, you'd have thought they were leaving a funeral. And Diego felt as if they were.

"Hey, D! D's home, Mom! Mom, D's home!" shouted Carlos as Diego wearily pushed the back door open. Carlos ran up to him, jumping up and down like a terrier puppy.

"Hi, Carlos," Diego just managed to say. Then he staggered over to the kitchen table and collapsed into a chair.

"How'd it go?" his mother asked him cautiously. "Not so great?"

"That's one way of putting it."

"Oh, well," his mother said, trying to comfort him. "You know what they say: a bad dress rehearsal means a good performance!"

"If that's true, then we're in for an award-winning performance," Diego muttered.

But he had a horrible feeling it wasn't going to work out that way.

# Chapter Ten

# *Planetary Peter Pan:* World Premiere

"I'm absolutely positive I'm going to throw up," Tiffany announced.

It was seven o'clock in the evening, and the hour of doom was at hand. At Hollis Elementary School, it always meant the hour of doom when Tiffany started telling people that she was about to throw up.

At eight o'clock, the curtain would rise and *Planetary Peter Pan* would be introduced to the world. And it was safe to say that the cast and crew of the play were not exactly ready to go on stage.

Diego and Bob were frantically helping the lighting crew to reposition the floodlights, which had gotten knocked over earlier in the day when the third-graders had been practicing their square dancing in the lunchroom. Tiffany was frantically slapping a second coat of paint onto the wall she'd rebuilt the night before. Chantilly was frantically coaching Bonnie and Steve Tobias through a scene that Bob had frantically rewritten that afternoon. Junior was frantically flopping around on his hands and knees trying to get his tail to wag. As for everyone else in the class, they were just hanging around generally looking frantic.

In the midst of all this frantic activity, Jennifer Stevens strolled backstage and dumped an armful of costumes onto the floor—or rather, an armful of almost costumes.

"I got them cut out," she said casually, "but I didn't quite get them put together. I thought maybe a couple of people could kind of, you know, pitch in and help me. Like you, Tiffany," she added. "You don't have any lines to memorize or anything."

"Jennifer, can't you see that I'm busy?" Tiffany practically shrieked. "If I don't finish painting this set, we'll have a big gray spot instead of the Darlings' house!"

"Oh, I see. I guess you *want* the costumes to fall off the people's backs during the play, is that it?" Jennifer said grumpily.

She sounds as if this whole thing is Tiffany's fault! Diego thought. Quickly, he stepped forward. "I'll finish painting the set, Tiffany," he said. "I can paint a lot faster than I can sew."

"Well, I'm glad *some* people around here care about this play," Jennifer snapped.

"And you can help me paint, Jennifer," added Diego. "I bet you paint a lot faster than you sew, too."

"Everything going okay here?" came a cheery voice as Mrs. Doubleday walked backstage. "No one's too nervous, right?"

"That depends what you mean by 'too,'" Chantilly said.

"Mrs. Doubleday, do you think you could give us a hand here?" Bonnie called in an urgent voice. "Tiffany just sewed the bottom of my dress shut by mistake."

"Oh, dear," said Mrs. Doubleday. "Here I come!"

"Okay," Chantilly said, when all the last-minute jobs had been finished. "I guess I better start inspiring the troops. Could everyone come over here?" she called.

As people gathered around, Diego noticed Rocky cramming a cheeseburger into his mouth. *Maybe he knows it will be his last after tonight*, he thought.

"Okay, guys," Chantilly said gently when everyone in the class was standing in front of her. "I know I got angry last night, but things are going to be different tonight. We're all going to do a great job. I can just feel it."

"*How* can you feel it?" quavered Tiffany.

"I just do," Chantilly answered stoutly. "We know our lines"—Diego noticed she refused to look at Rocky as she said that—"and we've got great special effects. What can go wrong?"

"Well, I can think of one thing," Tiffany said. "Could everyone please, please be sure not to touch the new set I made? The paint's not dry yet."

It was too bad that she didn't think of warning Louie Watson not to put his foot through the wall of the new set. Because that's exactly what he did just before the curtain went up.

"It's not a problem!" Chantilly said instantly. "We'll just...we'll just...we'll just make sure someone's standing in front of the hole all the time! Everybody make sure to stand there whenever you're on stage, okay? Great! Now, let's go out there and knock 'em dead! I don't really mean that, of course," she added quickly, looking at the Watson twins.

Peter, Wendy, John, Michael, and Nana were all on their way to Never-Neverland, but Captain Hook didn't know it yet. He was striding around the island getting his morning exercise—in other words, swiping at everything with his sword. Then he spotted something dark on the horizon ... something that was growing larger. As he realized who it was, his face twisted into a mask of hatred—and Rocky opened his mouth to say his first line.

But before he could say it, a whisper floated out from the wing where Chantilly was standing with a copy of the script in her hands. Diego was standing right next to her, ready to find her place if she lost it while prompting Rocky.

"'Ahoy, fellow pirates,'" she whispered loudly. But not loud enough for the audience to hear.

For a split second, Rocky stared confusedly into the wings. Then he turned back toward the audience and repeated, "'Ahoy, fellow pirates!'" And to Diego's amazement, he kept going.

"'I spy Peter Pan and Tinker Bell!'"

"'They'll not escape me this time,'" came Chantilly's whisper from the wings in the split second before Rocky continued. "'They'll not escape me this time!'"

And the two of them kept going, only a beat apart.

"'No, I'll ...'" "'No, I'll catch that little rapscallion and ...'" "'From limb to ...'" "'Limb, or my name isn't Captain...'" "'Hook!'" "'Hook!'"

Rocky stopped talking for a second and glared into the wings. "Cut it out!" he hissed at Chantilly. "I know my lines!"

"I think he really does know them!" Diego whispered to her. "You must have scared him so much that he actually decided to learn them!"

And Rocky didn't make a single mistake for the rest of the play.

"Why is everyone bunched up on the side like that?" Diego whispered to Chantilly a few minutes later.

"I guess they're trying to hide that hole in the set!" she mouthed back. "I didn't mean *everybody* had to do it! Do you think the audience is noticing?"

"I don't see how they can help it!" Diego said.

The hole Louie had kicked was way over on the side of the set—which meant that all the action was taking place way over on the side of the set, too. It was true that the hole didn't show now, but Diego wasn't sure it looked any better to have all twelve actors onstage huddling together as though they were keeping each other warm.

"Hey, Rocky! You're doing great. But tell everyone to move over a little!" he instructed when Rocky came backstage for a scene change.

"Okay." Rocky held out the laser sword he had just used onstage. "What do you want me to do with this? It's about to burn out, I think."

"Just throw it over there." Diego pointed to a spot in the corner. "There's no reason to save any of this stuff. We won't be needing it anymore."

"They sure loved it, though, didn't they?" Rocky said proudly.

And they had. Even with three-fourths of the stage empty of actors, the audience seemed to love the play—and especially Diego's special effects.

They gasped in wonder during the flying scenes. They shrieked in terror during the fight scenes. They roared their approval when Captain Hook disappeared down the crocodile's maw. And when at last the curtain came down, Diego had never heard so much cheering.

No one in the audience could see what was behind the curtain, of course. But if they could have peeked, they would have seen that there was just as much celebration going on backstage.

"We did it!" shouted Diego. "We did it!" Laughing, he reached down and picked up a shattered alien head. "The nightmare is over! We never have to do this again! I never have to design anymore of these *things* again!" And he threw the alien head to the floor, where it skittered apart into a pile of tiny plastic fragments.

"Rocky, you were fantastic," Diego went on. "The perfect Captain Hook."

"You really were, Rocky," Chantilly echoed. "I'm buying you a cheeseburger with my very own money after the show. Everyone was great. I'm so proud of you all. And I can't *believe* this is all over!"

Then they heard Mr. Haypence's booming voice on the other side of the curtain. "Attention, please!" he called. "Please! A moment of your time."

Gradually, the lunchroom quieted down again. *Mr. Haypence must be holding up his hand*, Diego thought. Then the principal spoke.

"I must confess something to all of you," he said. "As hard as it is for me to say it, I had my doubts about this play at first."

"Oh, no!" some kid in the audience called out jeeringly.

"Yes, yes," replied Mr. Haypence in a solemn voice. "Yes, indeed. I could hardly believe the beautiful old story of Peter Pan could be improved. But I'm always the first to admit it when I've made a mistake. And now I'm admitting it. *Planetary Peter Pan* is a triumph ... No, don't applaud again." He said this even though there had been no signs of applause. People almost never applauded when they heard Mr. Haypence make a speech, even if they agreed with him. It was too likely to make him talk even longer.

"*Planetary Peter Pan* is a triumph," he repeated, "and I'm going to prove it to everyone. And how am I going to do that?"

Behind the curtain, everyone in Diego's class stopped moving, and, maybe, even breathing....

"By taking this show on the road."

"Oh, no," Diego whispered.

"We're going to visit all the schools in the district and all the school boards. I want all those students to have a chance to see our new classic. And I know all of them will love that witty dialogue and those wonderful special effects as much as I do. We'll show them what Hollis students can do when they put their minds to it!"

There was a horrified silence backstage, and then Diego spoke.

"I guess it's time to break out the papier-mâché," he said.